T0368514

Dakota
the
Drum

AuthorHouse™
1663 Liberty Drive
Bloomington, IN 47403
www.authorhouse.com
Phone: 833-262-8899

Because of the dynamic nature of the Internet, any web addresses or links contained in this book may have changed
since publication and may no longer be valid. The views expressed in this work are solely those of the author and do not
necessarily reflect the views of the publisher, and the publisher hereby disclaims any responsibility for them.

Any people depicted in stock imagery provided by Getty Images are models,
and such images are being used for illustrative purposes only.
Certain stock imagery © Getty Images.

This book is printed on acid-free paper.

ISBN: 979-8-8230-3939-0 (sc)
ISBN: 979-8-8230-3940-6 (e)

Library of Congress Control Number: 2024927678

Print information available on the last page.

Published by AuthorHouse 03/06/2025

authorHOUSE®

Dakota the Drum

By: Cherry Steinwender
Illustrator: Muhammad Saqib Riaz

Message to all Children

You have the freedom to identify yourself in any way that feels right for you.

Janiva Henderson

"My name is Dakota and I'm a Drum.

"I live in the pantry of the Lendrix family. Everybody tells me 'You're not a drum. You're just a big old soup pot.' That makes me sad every time I hear it."

Lendrix Family Pictured Below

One day, Dakota decided to leave home

Dakota said goodbye to the pots and pans in the pantry and told them, "I'm going out into the world where I can be a Drum and make music."

Everywhere Dakota went, Dakota saw different kinds of bands. But none of them recognized Dakota as a drum.

Even the children Dakota met told Dakota, "You're not a drum. You're just a big old soup pot."

Finally, Dakota sat on the curb. Dakota felt so sad and discouraged. All Dakota wanted to do was to make music.

All of a sudden, a man and woman in a military uniform walked up to Dakota.

"Why are you so sad?" the military man asked Dakota.

"I'm sad because no one thinks I'm a drum," Dakota said.

"You can be part of my military band to lead people into war," the woman answered.

At first, Dakota was very excited but then Dakota thought about it for a minute.

"Thank you kind military people, but I don't want to play music to lead people into war," Dakota said.

Not long after that, Dakota heard music in the distance. Quickly Dakota left the curb to find it. Soon Dakota saw a street band. As Dakota moved closer to it, Dakota saw that it was a very special street band.

Instead of tambourines and other traditional musical instruments, this band was made up of trash cans, sticks, old water bottles and beads.

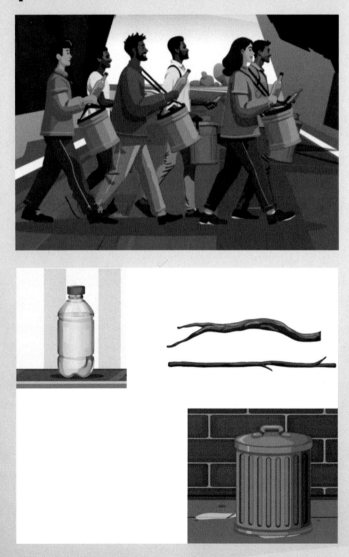

Dakota was amazed. The people in the band were using items they had found on the street to make music! And they were making the sounds of the city.

All of a sudden one of the street musicians noticed Dakota watching them. The musician thought Dakota looked like a perfect drum for the band. The musician quickly invited Dakota to join them. Dakota fit right in!

From that day forward, Dakota traveled the world with the "Sound of the City Band." But once a year Dakota would return to the Lendrix family and visit the pots, pans and skillets.

And every year when Dakota went home, the Lendrix family would invite their friends and relatives to come over for dinner. For just one day, Dakota chose to be a pot to make a big soup for everyone.

The End

Now it's your turn! Add your own stories...

Printed in the United States
by Baker & Taylor Publisher Services